S0-CPT-477

Writings of Harriet Beecher Stowe.

UNCLE TOM'S CABIN. *Popular Illustrated Edition.* 12mo, $2.00.

THE SAME. *Illustrated Edition.* A new edition, from new plates, printed with red-line border. With an Introduction of more than 30 pages, and a bibliography of the various editions and languages in which the work has appeared, by Mr. GEORGE BULLEN, of the British Museum. Over 100 illustrations. 8vo, $3.00.

THE SAME. *Popular Edition.* With Introduction, and Portrait of "Uncle Tom." 12mo, $1.00.

DRED (sometimes called "Nina Gordon"). 12mo, $1.50.

THE MINISTER'S WOOING. 12mo, $1.50.

AGNES OF SORRENTO. 12mo, $1.50.

THE PEARL OF ORR'S ISLAND. 12mo, $1.50.

THE MAY-FLOWER, ETC. 12mo, $1.50.

OLDTOWN FOLKS. 12mo, $1.50.

SAM LAWSON'S FIRESIDE STORIES. New and enlarged Edition. Illustrated. 12mo, $1.50.

MY WIFE AND I. New Edition. Illustrated. 12mo, $1.50.

WE AND OUR NEIGHBORS. New Edition. Illustrated. 12mo, $1.50.

POGANUC PEOPLE. New Edition. Illustrated 12mo, $1.50.

The above eleven 12mo volumes, uniform, in box, $16.00.

HOUSE AND HOME PAPERS. 16mo, $1.50.

LITTLE FOXES. 16mo, $1.50.

THE CHIMNEY-CORNER. 16mo, $1.50.

A DOG'S MISSION, ETC. New Edition. Illustrated. Small 4to, $1.25.

QUEER LITTLE PEOPLE. New Edition. Illustrated. Small 4to, $1.25.

LITTLE PUSSY WILLOW. New Edition. Illustrated. Small 4to, $1.25.

RELIGIOUS POEMS. Illustrated. 16mo, gilt edges, $1.50.

PALMETTO LEAVES. Sketches of Florida. Illustrated. 16mo, $1.50.

FLOWERS AND FRUIT. From Mrs. STOWE'S Writings. 16mo, $1.00.

SCENES FROM MRS. STOWE'S WORKS. Paper, 15 cents.

HOUGHTON, MIFFLIN & CO., *Publishers,*

BOSTON.

"'An't she a peart young un?' said Tom, holding her from him to take a full length view." —Page 29.

"'An't she a peart young un?' said Tom, holding her from him to take a full length view." — Page 29.

UNCLE TOM'S CABIN

OR, LIFE AMONG THE LOWLY

BY

HARRIET BEECHER STOWE

New Edition

WITH AN INTRODUCTORY ACCOUNT OF THE WORK
BY THE AUTHOR

BOSTON AND NEW YORK
HOUGHTON, MIFFLIN AND COMPANY
The Riverside Press, Cambridge
1890

The Riverside Press, Cambridge, Mass., U. S. A.
Electrotyped and Printed by H. O. Houghton & Company.

PREFACE.

The scenes of this story, as its title indicates, lie among a race hitherto ignored by the associations of polite and refined society; an exotic race, whose ancestors, born beneath a tropic sun, brought with them, and perpetuated to their descendants, a character so essentially unlike the hard and dominant Anglo-Saxon race, as for many years to have won from it only misunderstanding and contempt.

But, another and better day is dawning; every influence of literature, of poetry, and of art, in our times, is becoming more and more in unison with the great master chord of Christianity, "good-will to man."

The poet, the painter, and the artist now seek out and embellish the common and gentler humanities of life, and, under the allurements of fiction, breathe a humanizing and subduing influence, favorable to the development of the great principles of Christian brotherhood.

The hand of benevolence is everywhere stretched out, searching into abuses, righting wrongs, alleviating distresses, and bringing to the knowledge and sympathies of the world the lowly, the oppressed, and the forgotten.

In this general movement, unhappy Africa at last is remembered; Africa, who began the race of civilization and human progress in the dim, gray dawn of early time, but who, for centuries, has lain bound and bleeding at the foot of civilized and Christianized humanity, imploring compassion in vain.

But the heart of the dominant race, who have been her conquerors, her hard masters, has at length been turned towards her in mercy; and it has been seen how far nobler it is in nations to protect the feeble than to oppress them. Thanks be to God, the world has at last outlived the slave-trade!

The object of these sketches is to awaken sympathy and feeling for the African race, as they exist among us; to show their wrongs and sorrows, under a system so necessarily cruel and unjust as to defeat and do away the good effects of all that can be attempted for them, by their best friends, under it.

In doing this, the author can sincerely disclaim any invidious feeling towards those individuals who, often without any fault of their own, are involved in the trials and embarrassments of the legal relations of slavery.

Experience has shown her that some of the noblest of minds and hearts are often thus involved; and no one knows better than they do, that what may be gathered of the evils of slavery from sketches like these, is not the half that could be told, of the unspeakable whole.

In the Northern States, these representations may, perhaps, be thought caricatures; in the Southern States are witnesses who know their fidelity. What personal knowledge the author has had, of the truth of incidents such as here are related, will appear in its time.

It is a comfort to hope, as so many of the world's sorrows and wrongs have, from age to age, been lived down, so a time shall come when sketches similar to these shall be valuable only as memorials of what has long ceased to be.

When an enlightened and Christianized community shall have, on the shores of Africa, laws, language, and literature, drawn from among us, may then the scenes of the house of bondage be to them like the remembrance of Egpyt to the Israelite, — a motive of thankfulness to Him who hath redeemed them!

For, while politicians contend, and men are swerved this way and that by conflicting tides of interest and passion, the great cause of human liberty is in the hands of One, of whom it is said: —

> "He shall not fail nor be discouraged
> Till he have set judgment in the earth."
>
> "He shall deliver the needy when he crieth,
> The poor, and him that hath no helper."
>
> "He shall redeem their soul from deceit and violence,
> And precious shall their blood be in his sight."

TABLE OF CONTENTS.

INTRODUCTION

TO THE NEW EDITION.

The introduction of a new American Edition of "Uncle Tom's Cabin" gives an occasion for a brief account of that book, — how it came to be, how it was received in the world, and what has been its history throughout all the nations and tribes of the earth, civilized and uncivilized, into whose languages it has been translated.

Its author had for many years lived in Ohio on the confines of a slave state, and had thus been made familiar with facts and occurrences in relation to the institution of American slavery. Some of the most harrowing incidents related in the story had from time to time come to her knowledge in conversation with former slaves now free in Ohio. The cruel sale and separation of a married woman from her husband, narrated in Chapter XII., "Select Incident of Lawful Trade," had passed under her own eye while passenger on a steamboat on the Ohio River. Her husband and brother had once been obliged to flee with a fugitive slave woman by night, as described in Chapter IX., and she herself had been called to write the letters for a former slave woman, servant in her own family, to a slave husband in Kentucky, who, trusted with unlimited liberty, free to come and go on business between Kentucky and Ohio, still refused to break his pledge of honor to his master, though that master from year to year deferred the keeping of his promise of freedom to the slave. It was the simple honor and loyalty of this Christian black man, who remained in slavery rather than violate a trust, that first impressed her with the possibility of such a character as, years after, was delineated in Uncle Tom.

From time to time incidents were brought to her knowledge

which deepened her horror of slavery. In her own family she had a private school for her children, and as there was no provision for the education of colored children in her vicinity, she allowed them the privilege of attending. One day she was suddenly surprised by a visit from the mother of one of the brightest and most amusing of these children. It appeared that the child had never been emancipated, and was one of the assets of an estate in Kentucky, and had been seized and carried off by one of the executors, and was to be sold by the sheriff at auction to settle the estate. The sum for the little one's ransom was made up by subscription in the neighborhood, but the incident left a deep mark in Mrs. Stowe's mind as to the practical workings of the institution of slavery.

But it was not for many years that she felt any call to make use of the materials thus accumulating. In fact, it was a sort of general impression upon her mind, as upon that of many humane people in those days, that the subject was so dark and painful a one, so involved in difficulty and obscurity, so utterly beyond human hope or help, that it was of no use to read, or think, or distress one's self about it. There was a class of professed abolitionists in Cincinnati and the neighboring regions, but they were unfashionable persons and few in number. Like all asserters of pure abstract right as applied to human affairs, they were regarded as a species of moral monomaniacs, who, in the consideration of one class of interests and wrongs, had lost sight of all proportion and all good judgment. Both in church and in state they were looked upon as "those that troubled Israel."

It was a general saying among conservative and sagacious people that this subject was a dangerous one to investigate, and that nobody could begin to read and think upon it without becoming practically insane; moreover, that it was a subject of such delicacy that no discussion of it could be held in the free states without impinging upon the sensibilities of the slave states, to whom alone the management of the matter belonged.

So when Dr. Bailey — a wise, temperate, and just man, a model of courtesy in speech and writing — came to Cincinnati and set up an anti-slavery paper, proposing a fair discussion of the subject, there was an immediate excitement. On two occasions a mob led by slave-holders from Kentucky attacked his office, destroyed his printing-press, and threw his types into the Ohio River. The most of the Cincinnati respectability, in church and state, contented themselves on this occasion with reprobating the imprudence of Dr. Bailey in thus "arousing the passions of our fellow-citizens of Kentucky." In these mobs and riots the free colored people were threatened, maltreated, abused, and often had to flee for their lives. Even the servants of good families were often chased to the very houses of their employers, who rescued them with difficulty; and the story was current in those days of a brave little woman, who defended her black waiter, standing, pistol in hand, on her own doorstep, and telling the mob face to face that they should not enter except over her dead body.

Professor Stowe's house was more than once a refuge for frightened fugitives on whom the very terrors of death had fallen, and the inmates slept with arms in the house and a large bell ready to call the young men of the adjoining Institution, in case the mob should come up to search the house. Nor was this a vain or improbable suggestion, for the mob in their fury had more than once threatened to go up and set fire to Lane Seminary, where a large body of the students were known to be abolitionists. Only the fact that the Institution was two miles from the city, with a rough and muddy road up a long high hill, proved its salvation. Cincinnati mud, far known for its depth and tenacity, had sometimes its advantages.

The general policy of the leaders of society, in cases of such disturbances, was after the good old pattern in Judæa, where a higher One had appeared, who disturbed the traders in swine; "they besought him that he would depart out of their coasts." Dr. Bailey at last was induced to remove his paper to Washington, and to conduct his investigation under the protection of the national Capitol, — and there for years he demonstrated the fact that the truth may be spoken plainly yet courteously, and with all honorable and Christian fairness, on the most exciting of subjects. In justice to the south it must be said, that his honesty, courage, and dignity of character won for him friends even among the most determined slave-holders. Manly men have a sort of friendship for an open, honest opponent, like that of Richard Cœur de Lion for Saladin.

Far otherwise was the fate of Lovejoy, who essayed an anti-slavery paper at Alton, Illinois. A mob from Missouri besieged the office, set the house on fire, and shot him at the door. It was for some days reported that Dr. Beecher's son, Rev. Edward Beecher, known to have been associated with Lovejoy at this period, had been killed at the same time. Such remembrances show how well grounded were the fears which attended every effort to agitate this subject. People who took the side of justice and humanity in those days had to count the cost and pay the price of their devotion. In those times, when John G. Fee, a young Kentucky student in Lane Seminary, liberated his slaves, and undertook to preach the gospel of emancipation in Kentucky, he was chased from the state, and disinherited by his own father. Berea College, for the education of colored and white, stands to-day a triumphant monument of his persistence in well-doing. Mr. Van Zandt, a Kentucky farmer, set free his slaves and came over and bought a farm in Ohio. Subsequently, from an impulse of humanity, he received and protected fugitive slaves in the manner narrated in Chapter IX. of "Uncle Tom's Cabin." For this he was seized, imprisoned, his property attached, and he was threatened with utter ruin. Salmon P. Chase, then a rising young lawyer in Cincinnati, had the bravery to appear as his lawyer. As he was leaving the court-room, after making his plea, one of the judges remarked, "There goes a young man who has *ruined* himself to-day," and the sentiment was echoed by the general voice of society. The case went against Van Zandt, and Mr. Chase carried it up to the Supreme Court of the United States, which, utterly ignoring argument and justice, decided it against him. But a few years more, and Salmon P. Chase was himself Chief Justice of the United States. It was one of those rare dramatic instances in which courage and justice sometimes bring a reward even in this life.

After many years' residence in Ohio, Mrs. Stowe returned to make her abode in New England, just in the height of the excitement produced by the Fugitive Slave Law. Settled in Brunswick, Maine, she was in constant communication with friends in Boston, who wrote to her from day to day of the terror and despair which that law had occasioned to industrious, worthy colored people who had from time to time escaped to Boston, and were living in peace and security. She heard of families broken up and fleeing in the dead of winter to the frozen shores of Canada. But what seemed to her more inexplicable, more dreadful, was the apparent apathy of the Christian world of the free north to these proceedings. The pulpits that denounced them were exceptions; the voices raised to remonstrate few and far between.

In New England, as at the west, professed abolitionists were a small, despised, unfashionable band, whose constant remonstrances from year to year had been disregarded as the voices of impracticable fanatics. It seemed now as if the system once confined to the Southern States was rousing itself to new efforts to extend itself all over the north, and to overgrow the institutions of free society.

With astonishment and distress Mrs. Stowe heard on all sides, from humane and Christian people, that the slavery of the blacks was a guaranteed constitutional right, and that all opposition to it endangered the national Union. With this conviction she saw that even earnest and tender-hearted Christian people seemed to feel it a duty to close their eyes, ears, and hearts to the harrowing details of slavery, to put down all discussion of the subject, and even to assist slave-owners to recover fugitives in Northern States. She said to herself, these people cannot know what slavery is; they do not see what they are defending; and hence arose a purpose to write some sketches which should show to the world slavery as she had herself seen it. Pondering this subject, she was one day turning over a little bound volume of an anti-slavery magazine, edited by Mrs. Dr. Bailey, of Washington, and there she read the account of the escape of a woman with her child on the ice of the Ohio River from Kentucky. The incident was given by an eye-witness, one who had helped the woman to the Ohio shore. This formed the first salient point of the story. She began to meditate. The faithful slave husband in Kentucky occurred to her as a pattern of Uncle Tom, and the scenes of the story began gradually to form themselves in her mind.

The first part of the book ever committed to writing was the death of Uncle Tom. This scene presented itself almost as a tangible vision to her mind while sitting at the communion-table in the little church in Brunswick. She was perfectly overcome by it, and could scarcely restrain the convulsion of tears and sobbings that shook her frame. She hastened home and wrote it, and her husband being away she read it to her two sons of ten and twelve years of age. The little fellows broke out into convulsions of weeping, one of them saying, through his sobs, "Oh! mamma, slavery is the most cursed thing in the world!" From that time the story can less be said to have been composed by her than imposed upon her. Scenes, incidents, conversations rushed upon her with a vividness and importunity that would not be denied. The book insisted upon getting itself into being, and would take no denial. After the two or three first chapters were written, she wrote to Dr. Bailey of the "National Era" that she was planning a story that might probably run through several numbers of the "Era." In reply she received an instant application for it, and began immediately to send off weekly instalments. She was then in the midst of heavy domestic cares, with a young infant, with a party of pupils in her family to whom she was imparting daily lessons with her own children, and with untrained servants requiring constant supervision, but the story was so much more intense a reality to her than any other earthly thing that the weekly instalment never failed. It was there in her mind day and night waiting to be written, and requiring but a few moments to bring it into visible characters.

The weekly number was always read to the family circle before it was sent away, and all the household kept up an intense interest in the progress of the story.

As the narrative appeared in the "Era," sympathetic words began to come to her from old workers who had long been struggling in the anti-slavery cause. She visited Boston, went to the Anti-Slavery Rooms, and reinforced her *répertoire* of facts by such documents as Theodore D. Weld's "Slavery As It Is," the Lives of Josiah Henson and Lewis Clarke, particulars from both whose lives were inwoven with the story in the characters of Uncle Tom and George Harris.

In shaping her material the author had but one purpose, to show the institution of slavery truly, just as it existed. She had visited in Kentucky, had formed the acquaintance of people who were just, upright, and generous, and yet slave-holders. She had heard their views and appreciated their situation; she felt that justice required that their difficulties should be recognized and their virtues acknowledged. It was her object to show that the evils of slavery were the inherent evils of a bad *system*, and not always the fault of those who had become involved in it and were its actual administrators.

Then she was convinced that the presentation of slavery alone, in its most dreadful forms, would be a picture of such unrelieved horror and darkness as nobody could be induced to look at. Of set purpose, she sought to light up the darkness by humorous and grotesque episodes, and the presentation of the milder and more amusing phases of slavery, for which her recollection of the never-failing wit and drollery of her former colored friends in Ohio gave her abundant material. As the story progressed, a young publisher, J. P. Jewett, of Boston, set his eye upon it, and made overtures for the publication of it in book form, to which she consented. After a while she had a letter from him expressing his fears that she was making the story too long for a one-volume publication. He reminded her that it was an unpopular subject, and that people would not willingly hear much about it; that one short volume might possibly sell, but if it grew to two it might prove a fatal obstacle to its success. Mrs. Stowe replied that she did not make the story, that the story made itself, and that she could not stop it till it was done. The feeling that pursued her increased in intensity to the last, till with the death of Uncle Tom it seemed as if the whole vital force had left her. A feeling of profound discouragement came over her. Would anybody read it? Would anybody listen? Would this appeal, into which she had put heart, soul, mind, and strength, which she had written with her heart's blood, — would it, too, go for nothing, as so many prayers and groans and entreaties of these poor suffering souls had already gone? There had just been a party of slaves who had been seized and thrown into prison in Washington for a vain effort to escape. They were, many of them, partially educated, cultivated young men and women, to whom slavery was intolerable. When they were retaken and marched through the streets of Washington, followed by a jeering crowd, one of them, named Emily Edmundson, answered one man who cried shame upon her, that she was not ashamed, —

that she was proud that she and all the rest of them had made an effort for liberty! It was the sentiment of a heroine, but she and her sisters were condemned no less to the auction-block.

It was when the last proof-sheet had been sent to the office that Mrs. Stowe, alone and thoughtful, sat reading Horace Mann's eloquent plea for those young men and women, then about to be consigned to the slave warehouse of Bruin & Hill in Alexandria, — a plea eloquent, impassioned, but vain, as all other pleas on that side had ever proved in all courts hitherto. It seemed to her that there was no hope, that nobody would hear, nobody would read, nobody would pity; that this frightful system, which had already pursued its victims into the free states, might at last even threaten them in Canada.

So, determined to leave nothing undone which remotely could help the cause she pleaded, she wrote one letter to Prince Albert to accompany a copy of her work; another to T. B. Macaulay, of whose father she had heard in her youth as an anti-slavery laborer; one to Charles Dickens, whose sympathy for the slave had been expressed more than once; one to Charles Kingsley, and one to Lord Carlisle. These letters were dispatched to their destination with early copies of the book, and all in due time acknowledged to the author.

"Uncle Tom's Cabin" was published March 20, 1852. The despondency of the author as to the question whether anybody would read or attend to her appeal was soon dispelled. Ten thousand copies were sold in a few days, and over three hundred thousand within a year, and eight power-presses, running day and night, were barely able to keep pace with the demand for it. It was read everywhere, apparently, and by everybody, and she soon began to hear echoes of sympathy all over the land. The indignation, the pity, the distress, that had long weighed upon her soul seemed to pass off from her, and into the readers of the book.

The following note from a lady, an intimate friend, was a specimen of many which the post daily brought her: —

MY DEAR MRS. STOWE, — I sat up last night until long after one o'clock, reading and finishing "Uncle Tom's Cabin." I *could not* leave it any more than I could have left a dying child; nor could I restrain an almost hysterical sobbing for an hour after I laid my head upon my pillow. I thought I was a thoroughgoing abolitionist before, but your book has awakened so strong a feeling of indignation and of compassion, that I seem never to have had *any* feeling on this subject till now. But what can we do? Alas! alas! what *can* we do? This storm of feeling has been raging, burning like a very fire in my bones all the livelong night, and through all my duties this morning it haunts me, — I *cannot* away with it. Gladly would I have gone out in the midnight storm last night, and, like the blessed martyr of old, been stoned to death, if that could have rescued these oppressed and afflicted ones. But that would avail nothing. And now what am I doing? Just the most foolish thing in the world. Writing to you, who need no incitement; to you, who have spun from your very vitals this tissue of agony and truths; for I know, I feel, that there are burning drops of your heart's best blood here concentrated. To *you*, who need no encouragement or sympathy of mine, and whom I would not insult by praise, — Oh no, you stand on too high an eminence for praise; but methinks I see the prayers of the poor, the blessings of those who are ready to perish, gathering in clouds about you, and forming a halo round your beloved head. And surely the tears of gentle, sympathizing childhood, that are dropping about many a Christian hearthstone over the wrongs and cruelties depicted by you so touchingly, will water the sod and spring up in bright flowers at your feet. And better still, I *know*, — I see, in the flushing cheek, the clenched hand, and indignant eye of the young man, as he dashes down the book and paces the room to hide the tears that he is too proud to show, too powerless to restrain, that you are sowing seed which shall yet spring up to the glory of God, to the good of the poor slave, to the enfranchisement of our beloved though guilty country.

Mrs. Stowe at this period visited New York. It was just at the time of Jenny Lind's first visit to this country, when the young Swedish vocalist was the idol of the hour, and tickets to her concerts were selling at fabulous prices. Mrs. Stowe's friends, applying for tickets, found all sold; but, on hearing of the application, the cantatrice immediately sent Mrs. Stowe two tickets to two of the best seats in the house. In reply to Mrs. Stowe's note of thanks came this answer: —

May 23, 1852.

My dear Madam, — Allow me to express my most sincere thanks for your very kind letter, which I was very happy to receive.

You must feel and know what deep impression "Uncle Tom's

Cabin" has made upon every heart that can feel for the dignity of human existence; so I, with my miserable English, would not even try to say a word about the great excellency of that most beautiful book, but *I must* thank you for the great joy I have felt over that book.

Forgive me, my dear madam; it is a great liberty I take in thus addressing you, I know, but I have *so* wished to find an opportunity to pour out my thankfulness in a few words to you that I cannot help this intruding. I have the feeling about "Uncle Tom's Cabin" that great changes will take place by and by from the impression people receive out of it, and that the writer of that book can "fall asleep" to-day or to-morrow with the bright sweet conscience of having been a strong, powerful means, in the Creator's hand, of operating essential good in one of the most important questions for the welfare of our black *brethren.* God bless and protect you and yours, dear madam, and certainly God's hand will remain with a blessing over your head.

Once more, forgive my bad English and the liberty I have taken, and believe me to be, dear madam,

Yours most truly,

JENNY GOLDSCHMIDT, *née* LIND.

A more cheering result was in the testimony of many colored persons and fugitive slaves, who said to her, "Since that book has come out, everybody is good to us; we find friends everywhere. It 's wonderful how kind everybody is."

In one respect, Mrs. Stowe's expectations were strikingly different from fact. She had painted slave-holders as amiable, generous, and just. She had shown examples among them of the noblest and most beautiful traits of character; had admitted fully their temptations, their perplexities, and their difficulties, so that a friend of hers who had many relatives in the south wrote to her in exultation: "Your book is going to be the great pacificator; it will unite both north and south." Her expectation was that the professed abolitionists would denounce it as altogether too mild in its dealings with slave-holders. To her astonishment, it was the extreme abolitionists who received, and the entire south who rose up against it.

Whittier wrote to Garrison in May, 1852: —

"It did me good to see thy handwriting, friend William, reminding me of the old days when we fought the beasts at Ephesus together in Philadelphia. Ah me! I am no longer able to take active part in the conflicts and skirmishes which are preparing the way for the great battle of Armageddon, — the world-wide, final struggle between freedom and slavery, — but, sick or well, in the body or out, I shall be no unconcerned spectator. I bless God that, through the leadings of his Providence, I have a right to rejoice in the certain victory of the right.

"What a glorious work Harriet Beecher Stowe has wrought! *Thanks* for the Fugitive Slave Law! Better for slavery that law had never been enacted, for it gave occasion for 'Uncle Tom's Cabin'!"

In a letter from Garrison to Mrs. Stowe, he said that he estimated the value of anti-slavery writing by the abuse it brought. "Since 'Uncle Tom's Cabin' has been published," he adds, "all the defenders of slavery have let me alone, and are spending their strength in abusing you." In fact, the post-office began about this time to bring her threatening and insulting letters from the Legrees and Haleys of the slave-markets, — letters so curiously compounded of blasphemy, cruelty, and obscenity, that their like could only be expressed by John Bunyan's account of the speech of Apollyon, — "He spake as a dragon."

After a little, however, responses began to come from across the water. The author had sent copies to Prince Albert, to Charles Dickens, to T. B. Macaulay, to Kingsley, and to Lord Carlisle. The receipt of the copy sent to Prince Albert was politely acknowledged, with thanks, by his private secretary. Her letter is here given: —

To His Royal Highness Prince Albert:

The author of this work feels that she has an apology for presenting it to Prince Albert, because it concerns the great interests of humanity, and from those noble and enlarged views of human progress which she has at different times seen in his public speeches, she has inferred that he has an eye and a heart for all that concerns the development and welfare of the human family.

Ignorant of the forms of diplomatic address, and the etiquette of rank, may she be pardoned for speaking with the republican simplicity of her own country, as to one who possesses a nobility higher than that of rank or station.

This simple narrative is an honest attempt to enlist the sympathies both of England and America in the sufferings of an oppressed race, to whom in less enlightened days both England and America were unjust.

The wrong on England's past has been atoned in a manner worthy of herself, nor in all her strength and glory is there anything that adds such lustre to her name as the position she holds in relation to human freedom. (May America yet emulate her example!)

The appeal is in greater part, as it should be, to the writer's own country, but when fugitives by thousands are crowding British shores, she would enlist for them the sympathy of British hearts.

We, in America, have been told that the throne of earth's mightiest nation is now filled by one less adorned by all this world can give of power and splendor, than by a good and noble heart, — a heart ever ready to feel for the suffering, the oppressed, and the lowly.

The author is encouraged by the thought that beneath the royal insignia of England throbs that woman's and mother's heart. May she ask that he who is nearest to her would present to her notice this simple story. Should it win from her compassionate nature pitying thoughts for those multitudes of poor outcasts, who have fled for shelter to the shadow of her throne, it were enough.

May the blessing of God rest on the noble country from which America draws her lineage, and on *her* the Queen of it. Though all the thrones be shaken, may *hers*, founded deep in the hearts of her subjects, be established to her and *to her children*, through all generations! With deep respect,

HARRIET BEECHER STOWE.

BRUNSWICK, ME., *March* 20, 1852.

Her letter to Charles Dickens and his reply are as follows: —

TO THE AUTHOR OF "DAVID COPPERFIELD":

The Author of the following sketches offers them to your notice as the first writer in our day who turned the attention of the high to the joys and sorrows of the lowly. In searching out and embellishing the forlorn, the despised, the lonely, the neglected and forgotten, lies the true mission which you have performed for the world. There is a moral bearing in it that far outweighs the amusement of a passing hour. If I may hope to do only something like the same, for a class equally ignored and despised by the fastidious and refined of my country, I shall be happy. Yours very truly,

HARRIET BEECHER STOWE.

TAVISTOCK HOUSE, LONDON, *July* 17, 1852.

DEAR MADAM, — I have read your book with the deepest interest and sympathy, and admire, more than I can express to you, both the generous feeling which inspired it, and the admirable power with which it is executed.

If I might suggest a fault in what has so charmed me, it would be that you go too far and seek to prove too much. The wrongs and atrocities of slavery are, God knows! case enough. I doubt there being any warrant for making out the African race to be a great race, or for supposing the future destinies of the world to lie in that direction; and I think this extreme championship likely to repel some useful sympathy and support.

Your book is worthy of any head and any heart that ever inspired a book. I am much your debtor, and I thank you most fervently and sincerely. CHARLES DICKENS.

MRS. HARRIET B. STOWE.

The following is the letter addressed to Macaulay, and his reply: —

HON. T. B. MACAULAY:

One of the most vivid recollections of my early life is the enthusiasm excited by reading your review of Milton, an enthusiasm deepened as I followed successively your writings as they appeared. A desire to hold some communion with minds that have strongly swayed and controlled our own is, I believe, natural to every one, and suggested to my mind the idea of presenting to you this work. When a child between eight and ten years of age, I was a diligent reader of the "Christian Observer," and in particular of the articles in which the great battle was fought against the slave-trade. An impression was then made on my mind which will never be obliterated. A similar conflict is now convulsing this nation, — an agitation which every successive year serves to deepen and widen. In this conflict the wise and good of *other lands* can materially aid us.

The *public sentiment of Christianized humanity* is the last court of appeal in which the cause of a helpless race is to be tried, and nothing operates more sensibly on this country than the temperate and just expression of the sentiments of distinguished men in your own. Every such expression is a shot which strikes the citadel. There is a public sentiment on this subject in England which often expresses itself in a way which does far less good than it might if those who expressed it had a more accurate knowledge and a more skilful touch, and yet even that has done good, though it has done harm also. The public sentiment of nations is rising to be a power stronger than that of fleets and armies, and it needs to be skilfully and wisely guided. He who should direct the feelings of England on this subject wisely and effectively might do a work worthy of your father, of Clarkson and Wilberforce, and all those brave men who began the great conflict for God and humanity.

I much misjudge your mind and heart if the subject is one on which you can be indifferent, or can speak otherwise than justly, humanely, and effectively. Yours with deep respect,

HARRIET BEECHER STOWE.

BRUNSWICK, ME., *March* 20, 1852.

THE ALBANY, LONDON, *May* 20, 1852.

MADAM, — I sincerely thank you for the volumes which you have done me the honor to send me. I have read them — I cannot say with pleasure; for no work on such a subject can give pleasure, but with high respect for the talents and for the benevolence of the writer. I have the honor to be, madam,

Your most faithful servant,

T. B. MACAULAY.

In October of 1856 Macaulay wrote to Mrs. Stowe: —

"I have just returned from Italy, where your fame seems to throw that of all other writers into the shade. There is no place where 'Uncle Tom' (transformed into 'Il Zio Tom') is not to be found. By this time I have no doubt he has 'Dred' for a companion."

Soon after Macaulay's letter came to her, Mrs. Stowe began to receive letters from other distinguished persons expressing a far warmer sympathy with the spirit and motive of her work.

FROM LORD CARLISLE.

LONDON, *July* 8, 1852.

MADAM, — I have allowed some time to elapse before I thanked you for the great honor and kindness you did me in sending to me from yourself a copy of "Uncle Tom's Cabin." I thought it due to the subject of which I perceived that it treated not to send a mere acknowledgment, as I confess from a motive of policy I am apt to do upon the first arrival of a book. I therefore determined to read before I wrote.

Having thus read, it is not in the stiff and conventional form of compliment, still less in the technical language of criticism, that I am about to speak of your work. I return my deep and solemn thanks to Almighty God, who has led and enabled you to write such a book. I do feel, indeed, the most thorough assurance that, in his good Providence, such a book cannot have been written in vain. I have long felt that Slavery is by far the *topping* question of the world and age we live in, including all that is most thrilling in heroism and most touching in distress, — in short, the real Epic of the Universe. The self-interest of the parties most nearly concerned on the one hand, the apathy and ignorance of unconcerned observers on the other, have left these august pretensions to drop very much out of sight, and hence my rejoicing that a writer has appeared who will be read and must be felt, and that, happen what may to the transactions of slavery, they will no longer be suppressed.

I trust that what I have just said was not required to show the entire sympathy I entertain with respect to the main truth and leading scope of your high argument, but we live in a world only too apt to regard the accessories and accidents of a subject above its real and vital essence. No one can know so well as you how much the external appearance of the negro detracts from the romance and sentiment which undoubtedly might attach to his position and to his wrongs; and on this account it does seem to me proportionately important that you should have brought to your portraiture great grace of style, great power of language, a play of humor which relieves and lightens even the dark depth of the background which you were called upon to reveal, a force of pathos which, to give it the highest praise, does not lag behind all the dread reality, and, above all, a variety, a discrimination, and a truth in the delineation of character which, even to my own scanty and limited experience of the society you describe, accredits itself instantaneously and irresistibly. There is one point which, in face of all that your book has aimed at and achieved, I think of extremely slight importance, but which I will nevertheless just mention, if only to show that I have not been bribed into this fervor of admiration. I think, then, that whenever you speak of England and her institutions it is in a tone which fails to do them justice. I do not know what distinct charges you think could be established against our aristocracy and capitalists; but you generally convey the impression that the same oppressions in degree, though not in kind, might be brought home to them which are now laid to the charge of southern slave-holders. Exposed to the same ordeal, I grant they might very probably not stand the test better. All I contend for is, that the circumstances in which they are placed, and the institutions by which they are surrounded, make the parallel wholly inapplicable. I cannot but suspect that your view has been in many respects derived from composers of fiction and others among ourselves, who, writing with distinguished ability, have been more successful in delineating and dissecting the morbid features of our modern society than in detecting the principle which is at fault or suggesting the appropriate remedy. My own belief is — liable, if you please, to national bias — that our capitalists are very much the same sort of persons as your own in the Northern States, with the same mixtures and inequalities of motive and action. With respect to our aristocracy, I should really be tempted to say that, tried by their conduct on the question of Free Trade, they do not sustain an unfavorable comparison with your uppermost classes. I need not repeat how irrelevant, after all, I feel what I have said upon this head to be to the main issues included in your work. There is little doubt, too, that as a nation we have our special failings, and one of them probably is that we care too little about what other nations think of us. Nor can I wish my countrymen ever to forget that their own past history should prevent them from being forward in casting accusations at their transatlantic brethren on the subject of slavery. With great ignorance of its actual miseries and horrors, there is also among us great ignorance of the fearful perplexities and difficulties with which its solution could not fail to be attended. I feel, however, that there is a considerable difference between reluctant acquiescence in what you inherit from the past, and voluntary fresh enlargements and reinforcements of the system. For instance, I should not say that the mode in which such an enactment as the Fugitive Slave Law has been considered in this country has at all erred upon the side of overmuch indignation.

I need not detain you longer. I began my letter with returning thanks to Almighty God for the appearance of your work, and I offer my humble and ardent prayer to the same Supreme Source that it may have a marked agency in hastening the great consummation, which I should feel it a practical atheism not to believe must be among the unfulfilled purposes of the Divine Power and Love.

I have the honor to be, madam,

Your sincere admirer and well-wisher,

CARLISLE.

MRS. BEECHER STOWE.

FROM REV. CHARLES KINGSLEY.

EVERSLEY, *August* 12, 1852.

MY DEAR MADAM, — Illness and anxiety have prevented my acknowledging long ere this your kind letter and your book, which, if success be a pleasure to you, has a success in England which few novels, and certainly no American book whatsoever, ever had. I cannot tell you how pleased I am to see coming from across the Atlantic a really healthy indigenous growth, "autochthones," free from all second and third hand Germanisms and Italianisms, and all other unrealisms.

Your book will do more to take away the reproach from your great and growing nation than many platform agitations and speechifyings. Here there is but one opinion about it. Lord Carlisle (late Morpeth) assured me that he believed the book, independent of its artistic merit (of which hereafter), calculated to produce immense good, and he can speak better concerning it than I can, for I pay you a compliment in saying that I have actually not read it through. It is too painful, — I cannot bear the sight of misery and wrong that I can do nothing to alleviate. But I will read it through and reread it in due time, though when I have done so, I shall have nothing more to say than what every one says now, that it is perfect.

I cannot resist transcribing a few lines which I received this morning from an excellent critic: "To my mind it is the greatest novel ever written, and though it will seem strange, it reminded me in a lower sphere more of Shakespeare than anything modern I have ever read; not in the style, nor in the humor, nor in the pathos, — though Eva set me a crying worse than Cordelia did at sixteen, — but in the many-sidedness, and, above all, in that marvellous clearness of insight and outsight, which makes it seemingly impossible for her to see any one of her characters without showing him or her at once as a distinct man or woman different from all others."

I have a debt of personal thanks to you for the book, also, from a most noble and great woman, my own mother, a West-Indian, who in great sickness and sadness read your book with delighted tears. What struck her was the way in which you, first of all writers, she said, had dived down into the depths of the negro heart, and brought out his common humanity without losing hold for a moment of his race peculiarities. But I must really praise you no more to your face, lest I become rude and fulsome. May God bless and prosper you, and all you write, is the earnest prayer, and, if you go on as you have begun, the assured hope, of your faithful and obliged servant,

CHARLES KINGSLEY.

FROM THE EARL OF SHAFTESBURY.[1]

LONDON, *December* 14, 1852.

MADAM, — It is very possible that the writer of this letter may be wholly unknown to you. But whether my name be familiar to your ears, or whether you now read it for the first time, I cannot refrain from expressing to you the deep gratitude that I feel to Almighty God, who has inspired both your heart and your head in the composition of "Uncle Tom's Cabin."

[1] Formerly Lord Ashley.

It would be out of place here to enumerate the various beauties, singular, original, and lasting, which shine throughout the work. One conviction, however, is constantly present to my mind, — the conviction that the gospel alone can elevate the intellect, even to the highest point. None but a Christian believer could have composed "Paradise Lost." None but a Christian believer could have produced such a book as yours, which has absolutely startled the whole world, and impressed many thousands by revelations of cruelty and sin which give us an idea of what would be the uncontrolled dominion of Satan on this fallen earth.

Your character of Eva is true. I have, allowing for the difference in sex, and the influences of a southern as compared with a northern climate, seen such myself in zeal, simplicity, and overflowing affection to God and man. It pleases God to show, every now and then, such specimens of his grace, and then remove them before they are tarnished by the world.

You are right, too, about Topsy. Our Ragged Schools will afford you many instances of poor children, hardened by kicks, insults, and neglect, moved to tears and to docility by the first word of kindness. It opens new feelings, develops, as it were, a new nature, and brings the wretched outcast into the family of man. I live in hope — God grant it may rise to faith! — that this system is drawing to a close. It seems as though our Lord had sent out this book as the messenger before his face to prepare his way before him. It may be that these unspeakable horrors are now disclosed to drive us to the only "hope of all the ends of the earth," the second advent of our blessed Saviour. Let us continue, as St. Paul says, "fervent and instant in prayer," and may we at the great day of account be found, with millions of this oppressed race, among the sheep at the right hand of our common Lord and Master!

Believe me, madam, with deep respect,

Your sincere admirer and servant,

SHAFTESBURY.

MRS. HARRIET BEECHER STOWE.

About the same time with this, Mrs. Stowe received a letter from Hon. Arthur Helps, accompanying a review of her work, written by himself, in a leading periodical. The main subject of Mr. Helps's letter was the one already alluded to in Lord Carlisle's letter, on the relation of the capitalists and higher classes of England to the working-classes, as compared with the relations of slave-holders and slaves in America. Her reply to this letter being shown to Archbishop Whately, she was surprised by a letter from him to the following purport: —

MADAM, — The writer of the article in "Fraser's Magazine" has favored me with a copy of your most interesting letter to him, and from it I collect that you will be glad to learn that I have been negotiating for the insertion of articles by very able hands on your truly valuable work in the "Edinburgh Review" and the "North British," both which are of wider circulation and more influence than that magazine.

The subject was discussed at the Statistical Section, of which I was president, of the British Association meeting in Belfast, and I then took occasion to call attention to your work.

It became evident, then, that the book had found powerful support and sympathy on English shores.

Sampson Low, who afterwards became Mrs. Stowe's English publisher, thus records its success in England: —

"From April to December, 1852, twelve different editions (not reissues) at one shilling were published, and within the twelve months of its first appearance no less than eighteen different houses in London were engaged in supplying the demand that had set in. The total number of editions was forty, varying from the fine illustrated edition of 15*s.* to the cheap popular one at 6*d.*

"After carefully analyzing these editions and weighing probabilities with ascertained facts, I am able pretty confidently to say that the aggregate number circulated in Great Britain and her colonies exceeded one million and a half."

Meanwhile Mrs. Stowe received intelligence of its appearance in Sweden from the pen of the accomplished Frederika Bremer.

FROM FREDERIKA BREMER.

STOCKHOLM, *January* 4, 1853.

MY DEAREST LADY, — How shall I thank you for your most precious, most delightful gift? Could I have taken your hand many a time, while I was reading your work, and laid it on my beating heart, you would have known the joy, the happiness, the exultation, it made me experience! It was the work I had long wished for, that I had anticipated, that I wished while in America to have been able to write, that I thought must come in America, as the uprising of the woman's and mother's heart on the question of slavery. I wondered that it had not come earlier. I wondered that the woman, the *mother*, could look at these things and be silent, — that no cry of noble indignation and anger would escape her breast, and rend the air, and pierce to the ear of humanity. I wondered, and, God be praised! it has come.

The woman, the mother, has raised her voice out of the very soil of the new world in behalf of the wronged ones, and her voice vibrates still through two great continents, opening all hearts and minds to the light of truth.

How happy you are to have been able to do it so well, to have been able to win all hearts while you so daringly proclaimed strong and bitter truths, to charm while you instructed, to amuse while you defended the cause of the little ones, to touch the heart with the softest sorrow while you aroused all our boldest energies against the powers of despotism.

In Sweden your work has been translated and published, as feuilleton in our largest daily paper, and has been read, enjoyed, and praised by men and women of all parties as I think no book here has been enjoyed and praised before. . . . I look upon you as a heroine who has won the battle. I think it is won! I have a deep unwavering faith in the strong humanity of the American mind. It will ever work to throw out whatever is at war with that humanity; and to make it fully alive, nothing is needed but a truly strong appeal of heart to heart, and that has been done in "Uncle Tom."

You have done it, dear, blessed, happy lady. Receive in these poor words my congratulations, my expressions of love and joy, my womanly pride in you as my sister in faith and love. God bless you forever!

FREDERIKA BREMER.

The author also received letters from France, announcing the enthusiastic reception of her work there. Madame George Sand, then one of the greatest powers of the literary world of France, thus introduced it to the public: —

To review a book the very morrow after its appearance, in the very journal where it has just been published, is doubtless contrary to usage, but in this case it is the most disinterested homage that can be rendered, since the immense success attained by this work at its publication does not need to be set forth.

This book is in all hands and in all journals. It has, and will have, editions in every form; people devour it, they cover it with tears. It is no longer permissible to those who can read not to have read it, and one mourns that there are so many souls condemned never to read it, — helots of poverty, slaves through ignorance, for whom society has been unable as yet to solve the double problem of uniting the food of the body with the food of the soul.

It is not, then, it cannot be, an officious and needless task to review this book of Mrs. Stowe. We repeat, it is a homage, and never did a generous and pure work merit one more tender and spontaneous. She is far from us; we do not know her who has penetrated our hearts with emotions so sad and yet so sweet. Let us thank her the more. Let the gentle voice of woman, the generous voice of man, with the voices of little children, so adorably glorified in this book, and those of the oppressed of this old world, let them cross the seas and hasten to say to her that she is esteemed and beloved!

If the best eulogy which one can make of the author is to love her, the truest that one can make of the book is to love its very faults. It has faults, — we need not pass them in silence, we need not evade the discussion of them, — but you need not be disturbed about them, you who are rallied on the tears you have shed over the fortunes of the poor victims in a narrative so simple and true.

These defects exist only in relation to the conventional rules of art, which never have been and never will be absolute. If its judges, possessed with the love of what they call "artistic work," find unskilful treatment in the book, look well at them to see if their eyes are dry when they are reading this or that chapter.

They will recall to your mind that Ohio senator, who, having sagely demonstrated to his little wife that it is a political duty to refuse asylum and help to the fugitive slave, ends by taking two in his own carriage, in a dark night, over fearful roads, where he must from time to time plunge into mud to his waist to push on the vehicle. This charming episode in "Uncle Tom" (a digression, if you will) paints well the situation of most men placed between their prejudices and established modes of thought and the spontaneous and generous intuitions of their hearts.

It is the history, at the same time affecting and pleasing, of many independent critics. Whatever they may be in the matter of social or literary questions, those who pretend always to judge by strict rules are often vanquished by their own feelings, and sometimes vanquished when unwilling to avow it.

I have always been charmed by the anecdote of Voltaire, ridiculing and despising the fables of La Fontaine, seizing the book and saying, "Look here, now, you will see in the very first one" — he reads one. "Well, that is passable, but see how stupid this is!" — he reads a second, and finds after all that it is quite pretty; a third disarms him again, and at last he throws down the volume, saying, with ingenuous spite, "It 's nothing but a collection of masterpieces." Great souls may be bilious and vindictive, but it is impossible for them to remain unjust and insensible.

It, however, should be said to people of culture, who profess to be able to give correct judgments, that if their culture is of the truest kind it will never resist a just and right emotion. Therefore it is that this book, defective according to the rules of the modern French romance, intensely interests everybody and triumphs over all criticisms in the discussions it causes in domestic circles.

For this book is essentially domestic and of the family, — this book, with its long discussions, its minute details, its portraits carefully studied. Mothers of families, young girls, little children, servants even, can read and understand them, and men themselves, even the most superior, cannot disdain them. We do not say that the success of the book is because its great merits redeem its faults ; we say its success is because of these very alleged faults.

For a long time we have striven in France against the prolix explanations of Walter Scott. We have cried out against those of Balzac, but on consideration have perceived that the painter of manners and character has never done too much, that every stroke of the pencil was needed for the general effect. Let us learn then to appreciate all kinds of treatment, when the effect is good, and when they bear the seal of a master hand.

Mrs. Stowe is all instinct ; it is the very reason that she appears to some not to have talent. Has she not talent ? What is talent ? Nothing, doubtless, compared to genius ; but has she genius ? I cannot say that she has talent as one understands it in the world of letters, but she has genius, as humanity feels the need of genius, — the genius of goodness, not that of the man of letters, but of the saint. Yes, — a saint ! Thrice holy the soul which thus loves, blesses, and consoles the martyrs. Pure, penetrating, and profound the spirit which thus fathoms the recesses of the human soul. Noble, generous, and great the heart which embraces in her pity, in her love, an entire race, trodden down in blood and mire under the whip of ruffians and the maledictions of the impious.

Thus should it be, thus should we value things ourselves. We should feel that genius is *heart*, that power is *faith*, that talent is *sincerity*, and, finally, success is *sympathy*, since this book overcomes us, since it penetrates the breast, pervades the spirit, and fills us with a strange sentiment of mingled tenderness and admiration for a poor negro lacerated by blows, prostrate in the dust, there gasping on a miserable pallet, his last sigh exhaled towards God.

In matters of art there is but one rule, to paint and to move. And where shall we find creations more complete, types more vivid, situations more touching, more original, than in "Uncle Tom," — those beautiful relations of the slave with the child of his master, indicating a state of things unknown among us ; the protest of the master himself against slavery during that innocent part of life when his soul belongs to God alone? Afterwards, when society takes him, the law chases away God, and interest deposes conscience. In coming to mature years the infant ceases to be *man* and becomes master. God dies in his soul.

What hand has ever drawn a type more fascinating and admirable than St. Clare, — this exceptional nature, noble, generous, and loving, but too soft and too nonchalant to be really great? Is it not man himself, human nature itself, with its innate virtues, its good aspirations, and its deplorable failures? — this charming master who loves and is beloved, who thinks and reasons, but concludes nothing and does nothing! He spends in his day treasures of indulgence, of consideration, of goodness; he dies without having accomplished anything. The story of his precious life is all told in a word — "to aspire and to regret." He has never learned to *will*. Alas! is there not something of this even among the bravest and best of men?

The life and death of a little child and of a negro slave! — that is the whole book! This negro and this child are two saints of heaven! The affection that unites them, the respect of these two perfect ones for each other, is the only love-story, the only passion of the drama. I know not what other genius but that of sanctity itself could shed over this affection and this situation a charm so powerful and so sustained. The child reading the Bible on the knees of the slave, dreaming over its mysteries and enjoying them in her exceptional maturity; now covering him with flowers like a doll, and now looking to him as something sacred, passing from tender playfulness to tender veneration, and then fading away through a mysterious malady which seems to be nothing but the wearing of pity in a nature too pure, too divine, to accept earthly law; dying finally in the arms of the slave, and calling him after her to the bosom of God, — all this is so new, so beautiful, that one asks one's self in thinking of it whether the success which has attended the work is after all equal to the height of the conception.

Children are the true heroes of Mrs. Stowe's works. Her soul, the most motherly that could be, has conceived of these little creatures in a halo of grace. George Shelby, the little Harry, the cousin of Eva, the regretted babe of the little wife of the Senator, and Topsy, the poor diabolic, excellent Topsy, — all the children that one sees, and even those that one does not see in this romance, but of whom one has only a few words from their desolate mothers, seem to us a world of little angels, white and black, where any mother may recognize some darling of her own, source of her joys and tears. In taking form in the spirit of Mrs. Stowe, these children, without ceasing to be children, assume ideal graces, and come at last to interest us more than the personages of an ordinary love-story.

Women, too, are here judged and painted with a master hand; not merely mothers who are sublime, but women who are not mothers either in heart or in fact, and whose infirmities are treated with indulgence or with rigor. By the side of the methodical Miss Ophelia, who ends by learning that duty is good for nothing without love, Marie St. Clare is a frightfully truthful portrait. One shudders in thinking that she exists, that she is everywhere, that each of us has met her and seen her, perhaps, not far from us, for it is only necessary that this charming creature should have slaves to torture, and we should see her revealed complete through her vapors and her nervous complaints.

The saints also have their claw! it is that of the lion. She buries it deep in the conscience, and a little of burning indignation and of terrible sarcasm does not, after all, misbecome this Harriet Stowe, this woman so gentle, so humane, so religious, and full of evangelical unction. Ah! yes, she is a very good woman, but not what we derisively call "goody good." Hers is a heart strong and courageous, which in blessing the unhappy and applauding the faithful, tending the feeble and succoring the irresolute, does not hesitate to bind to the pillory the hardened tyrant, to show to the world his deformity.

She is, in the true spirit of the word, consecrated. Her fervent Christianity sings the praise of the martyr, but permits no man the right to perpetuate the wrong. She denounces that strange perversion of Scripture which tolerates the iniquity of the oppressor because it gives opportunity for the virtues of the victims. She calls on God himself, and threatens in his name; she shows us human law on one side, and God on the other!

Let no one say that, because she exhorts to patient endurance of wrong, she justifies those who do the wrong. Read the beautiful page where George Harris, the white slave, embraces for the first time the shores of a free territory, and presses to his heart wife and child, who at last are *his own*. What a beautiful picture, that! What a large heart-throb! what a triumphant protest of the eternal and inalienable right of man to liberty!

Honor and respect to you, Mrs. Stowe! Some day your recompense, which is already recorded in heaven, will come also in this world. GEORGE SAND.

NOHANT, *December* 17, 1852.

Madame L. S. Belloc, also a well-known and distinguished writer, the translator of Miss Edgeworth's and of other English works into French, says: —

"When the first translation of 'Uncle Tom' was published in Paris there was a general hallelujah for the author and for the cause. A few weeks after, M. Charpentier, one of our best publishers, called on me to ask a new translation. I objected that there were already so many it might prove a failure. He insisted, saying, 'Il n'y aura jamais assez de lecteurs pour un tel livre,' and he particularly desired a special translation for his own collection, 'Bibliothèque Charpentier,' where it is catalogued, and where it continues now to sell daily. 'La Case de l'Oncle Tom' was the fifth, if I recollect rightly, and a sixth illustrated edition appeared some months after. It was read by high and low, by grown persons and children. A great enthusiasm for the anti-slavery cause was the result. The popularity of the work in France was immense, and no doubt influenced the public mind in favor of the north during the war of secession."

The next step in the history of "Uncle Tom" was a meeting at Stafford House, when Lord Shaftesbury recommended to the women of England the sending of an "affectionate and Christian address to the women of America."

This address, composed by Lord Shaftesbury, was taken in hand for signatures by energetic canvassers in all parts of England, and also among resident English on the Continent. The demand for signatures went as far forth as the city of Jerusalem. When all the signatures were collected, the document was forwarded to the care of Mrs. Stowe in America, with a letter from Lord Carlisle, recommending it to her, to be presented to the ladies of America in such way as she should see fit.

It was exhibited first at the Boston Anti-slavery fair, and now remains in its solid oak case a lasting monument of the feeling called forth by "Uncle Tom's Cabin."

It is in twenty-six thick folio volumes, solidly bound in morocco, with the American eagle on the back of each. On the first page of the first volume is the address, beautifully illuminated on vellum, and following are the subscribers' names, filling the volumes. There are 562,448 names of women of every rank of life, from the nearest in rank to the throne of England to the wives and daughters of the humblest artisan and laborer. Among all who signed, it is fair to presume there was not one who had not read the book, and did not, at the time of signing, feel a sympathy for the cause of the oppressed people whose wrongs formed its subject. The address, with its many signatures, was simply a relief to that impulsive desire to *do* something for the cause of the slave, which the reading of "Uncle Tom's Cabin" appeared to inspire.

Of the wisdom of this step there have been many opinions. Nobody, however, can doubt that Lord Shaftesbury, who had spent a long life in labors to lift burdens from the working-classes of England, and who had redeemed from slavery and degradation English women and children in its mines and collieries, had thereby acquired a certain right to plead for the cause of the oppressed working-classes in all countries.

The address was received as a welcome word of cheer and encouragement by that small band of faithful workers who for years had stood in an unfashionable minority; but so far as the feeling expressed in it was one of real Christian kindliness and humility, it was like a flower thrown into the white heat of a furnace. It added intensity, if that were possible, to that terrific conflict of forces which was destined never to cease till slavery was finally abolished.

It was a year after the publication of "Uncle Tom" that Mrs. Stowe visited England, and was received at Stafford House, there meeting all the best known and best worth knowing of the higher circles of England.

The Duchess of Sutherland, then in the height of that majestic beauty and that noble grace of manner which made her a fit representative of English womanhood, took pleasure in showing by this demonstration the sympathy of the better class of England with that small unpopular party in the United States who stood for the rights of the slave.

On this occasion she presented Mrs. Stowe with a solid gold bracelet made in the form of a slave's shackle, with the words, "We trust it is a memorial of a chain that is soon to be broken." On two of the links were inscribed the date of the abolition of the slave-trade, March 25, 1807, and of slavery in English territory, August 1, 1834. On another link was recorded the number of signatures to the address of the women of England.

At the time such a speech and the hope it expressed seemed like a Utopian dream. Yet that bracelet has now inscribed upon its other links the steps of American emancipation:

"Emancipation in District of Columbia, April 16, 1862;" "President's proclamation abolishing slavery in rebel states, January 1, 1863;" "Maryland free, October 13, 1864;" "Missouri free, January 11, 1865." "Constitutional amendment" (forever abolishing slavery in the United States) is inscribed on the clasp of the bracelet. Thus what seemed the vaguest and most sentimental possibility has become a fact of history.

A series of addresses presented to Mrs. Stowe at this time by public meetings in different towns of England, Scotland, and Ireland, still remain among the literary curiosities relating to this book. The titles of these are somewhat curious: "Address from the Inhabitants of Berwick-upon-Tweed;" "Address from the Inhabitants of Dalkeith;" "Address from the Committee of the Glasgow Female Anti-slavery Society;" "Address from the Glasgow University Abstainers' Society;" "Address from a Public Meeting in Belfast, Ireland;" "Address from the Committee of the Ladies' Anti-slavery Society, Edinburgh;" "Address from the City of Leeds."

All these public meetings, addresses, and demonstrations of sympathy were, in their time and way, doubtless of perfect sincerity. But when the United States went into a state of civil war, these demonstrations ceased.

But it is due to the brave true working-classes of England to say that in this conflict, whenever they thought the war was one of justice to the slave, they gave it their sympathy, and even when it brought hardship and want to their very doors, refused to lend themselves to any popular movement which would go to crush the oppressed in America.

It is but justice also to the Duchess of Sutherland to say, that although by the time our war was initiated she had retired from her place as leader of society to the chamber of the invalid, yet her sympathies expressed in private letters ever remained true to the cause of freedom.

Her son-in-law, the Duke of Argyll, stood almost alone in the House of Lords in defending the cause of the Northern States. It is, moreover, a significant fact that the Queen of England, in concurrence with Prince Albert, steadily resisted every attempt to enlist the warlike power of England against the Northern States.

But Almighty God had decreed the liberation of the African race, and though Presidents, Senators, and Representatives united in declaring that such were not *their* intentions, yet by great signs and mighty wonders was this nation compelled to listen to the voice that spoke from heaven, — "Let my people go."

In the darkest hour of the war, when defeat and discouragement had followed the Union armies, and all hearts were trembling with fear, Mrs. Stowe was in the Senate-Chamber at Washington, and heard these words in the Message of President Lincoln: —

"If this struggle is to be prolonged till there be not a house in the land where there is not one dead, till all the treasure amassed by the unpaid labor of the slave shall be wasted, till every drop of blood drawn by the lash shall be atoned by blood drawn by the sword, — we can only bow and say, 'Just and true are thy ways, thou King of Saints!'"

Such words were a fit exponent of the Emancipation Proclamation, which, though sown in weakness, was soon raised in power, and received the evident benediction of God's providence.

"Uncle Tom's Cabin," in the fervor which conceived it, in the feeling which it inspired through the world, was only one of a line of ripples marking the commencement of mighty rapids, moving by forces which no human power could stay to an irresistible termination, — towards human freedom.

Now the war is over, slavery is a thing of the past; slave-pens, blood-hounds, slave-whips, and slave-coffles are only bad dreams of the night; and now the humane reader can afford to read "Uncle Tom's Cabin" without an expenditure of torture and tears.

For many years Mrs. Stowe has had a home in the Southern States, and she has yet to meet an intelligent southern man or woman who does not acquiesce in the extinction of slavery, and feel that the life of free society is as great an advantage to the whites as to the blacks. Slavery has no mourners; there is nobody who wishes it back.

As to the influence of "Uncle Tom's Cabin" in various other lands of the earth whither it has been carried, intelligence has sometimes come to the author through the American missionaries and other sources. The three following letters are specimens.

In a letter from Miss Florence Nightingale, October 26, 1856, she says: —

"I hope it may be some pleasure to you, dear madam, to hear that 'Uncle Tom' was read by the sick and suffering in our Eastern Military Hospitals with intense interest. The interest in that book raised many a sufferer who, while he had not a grumble to bestow upon his own misfortunes, had many a thought of sorrow and just indignation for those which you brought before him. It is from the knowledge of such evils so brought home to so many honest hearts that they feel as well as know them, that we confidently look to their removal in God's good time."

From the Armenian Convent in the Lagoon of Venice came a most beautiful Armenian translation of "Uncle Tom," with a letter from the principal translator.

Rev. Mr. Dwight thus wrote to Professor Stowe from Constantinople, September 8, 1855: —

"'Uncle Tom's Cabin' in the Armenian language! Who would have thought it? I do not suppose your good wife, when she wrote that book, thought that she was going to missionate it among the sons of Haig in all their dispersions, following them along the banks of the Euphrates, sitting down with them in their towns and villages under the shade of hoary Ararat, travelling with them in their wanderings even to India and China. But I have it in my hands! in the Armenian of the present day, the same language in which I speak and think and dream. Now do not suppose this is any of *my* work, or that of any missionary in the field. The translation has been made and book printed at Venice by a fraternity of Catholic Armenian Monks perched there on the Island of St. Lazarus. It is in two volumes, neatly printed and with plates, I think translated from the French. It has not been in any respect materially altered, and when it is so, not on account of religious sentiment. The account of the negro prayer and exhortation meetings is given in full, though the translator, not knowing what we mean by people's becoming Christians, took pains to insert at the bottom of the page that at these meetings of the negroes great effects were sometimes produced by the warm-hearted exhortations and prayers, and it often happened that heathen negroes embraced Christianity on the spot.

One of your former scholars is now in my house, studying Armenian, and the book which I advised him to take as the best for the language is this 'Uncle Tom's Cabin.'"

Two or three other letters will conclude this *répertoire.*

86 Sauchiehall Street, Glasgow, *April* 16, 1853.

Mrs. H. B. Stowe:

Madam, — When persons of every rank in this country are almost vying with each other who is to show you most respect, you might perhaps think but little at being addressed by an exile, who offers you his heartfelt thanks, not for the mere gratification which the reading of "Uncle Tom's Cabin" afforded, but for the services you have rendered to the cause of humanity and of my country. You may be surprised at hearing of services rendered to my country (Poland); yet so it is. The unvarnished tale you published cannot fail to awaken the nobler feelings of man in every reader; it instils into their minds that fundamental Christian precept to love our fellow-beings; and it is by the spread of universal benevolence and not by revolutions that the cause of humanity is best promoted.

But you have done more than that, although you may be unconscious of it. A mother yourself, you have given comfort to other mothers. That foreign land where such pure benevolence as is taught in "Uncle Tom's Cabin" is honored cannot be a bad land; and though letters from their children do not always reach Polish mothers, your book is accessible to them, and gives them the conviction that their offspring, far as they are from them, are still within reach of maternal feelings.

A still higher good you have done to many a man by the picture of the patient faith of Uncle Tom. It was the custom of some persons to sneer at faith, on the supposition that it implied a blind belief in all that the clergyman utters. Your book has helped to dispel that delusion, and faith begins to be seen by some as something nobler, as the firm conviction of the mind that higher aims are placed before man than the gratification of his appetites and desires; that it is, in short, that strength of mind which restrains him from doing evil when his bad passions lead him into temptation.

I cannot address you in the name of a body, but as an exile, as a man belonging to the family of mankind, I beg to offer you my thanks and my wishes. May God bless you, may your days be many and prosperous, and may the noble aim you proposed yourself in writing "Uncle Tom's Cabin" be speedily accomplished! If I may add a request, I would beg of you to pray now and then for the poor Polish mothers, — a good person's prayer may be acceptable.

I am, madam, your most obedient servant,

Charles F. Müller.

WAVERLEY IN BELMONT, *October* 26, 1860.

MRS. H. B. STOWE:

DEAR MADAM, — I will not make any apology for the liberty which I take of writing to you, although I cannot claim any personal acquaintance. At any rate, I think you will excuse me. The facts which I wish to communicate will, I doubt not, be of sufficient interest to justify me.

It was my privilege, for such I shall esteem it on many accounts, to receive into my family and have under my especial care the young Brahmin whose recent visit to this country you must be acquainted with. I mean Joguth Chunder Gangooly, the first and only individual of his caste who has visited this country. Being highly intelligent and familiar with the social and intellectual character of the Hindoos of his native land, he gave me much information for which, in my scanty knowledge of that country, I was unprepared. Among other things he assured me that "Uncle Tom's Cabin" was a book as well known and as much read in Bengal among his own people as here in America, that it had been translated into their language, and been made a household book. He himself showed a familiar acquaintance with its contents, and assured me that it had done not a little to deepen the loathing of slavery in the minds of the Hindoos, and also to qualify their opinion of our country.

The facts which he gave me I believe to be substantially true, and deemed them such as would have an interest for the author of the book in question. Though I grieve for the wrong and shame which disgraces my country, I take a laudable pride in those productions of the true-hearted that appeal to the sympathies of all nations, and find a ready response in the heart of humanity.

With high respect,

Yours truly,

JAMES THURSTON.

From MRS. LEONOWENS, *formerly English Governess in the Family of the King of Siam.*

48 INGLIS STREET, HALIFAX, NOVA SCOTIA,
October 15, 1878.

MRS. H. B. STOWE:

DEAR MADAM, — The following is the fact, the result of the translation of "Uncle Tom's Cabin" into the Siamese language, by my friend, Sonn Klean, a lady of high rank at the court of Siam. I inclose it to you here, as related in one of my books.

"Among the ladies of the harem I knew one woman who more than all the rest helped to enrich my life, and to render fairer and more beautiful every lovely woman I have since chanced to meet. Her name translated itself, and no other name could have been more appropriate, into 'Hidden Perfume.' Her dark eyes were clearer and calmer, her full lips had a stronger expression of tenderness about them, and her brow, which was at times smooth and open, and at others contracted with pain, grew nobler and more beautiful as through her studies in English the purposes of her life strengthened and grew deeper and broader each day. Our daily lessons and translations from English into Siamese had become a part of her happiest hours. The first book we translated was 'Uncle Tom's Cabin,' and it soon became her favorite book. She would read it over and over again, though she knew all the characters by heart and spoke of them as if she had known them all her life. On the 3d of January, 1867, she voluntarily liberated all her slaves, men, women, and children, one hundred and thirty in all, saying, 'I am wishful to be good like Harriet Beecher Stowe, and never again to buy human bodies, but only to let them go free once more.' Thenceforth, to express her entire sympathy and affection for the author of 'Uncle Tom's Cabin,' she always signed herself Harriet Beecher Stowe; and her sweet voice trembled with love and music whenever she spoke of the lovely American lady who had taught her as even Buddha had taught kings to respect the rights of her fellow-creatures."

I remain,

Yours very truly,

A. H. LEONOWENS.

The distinctively religious influence of "Uncle Tom's Cabin" has been not the least remarkable of the features of its history.

Among other testimonials in the possession of the writer is a Bible presented by an association of workingmen in England on the occasion of a lecture delivered to them on "Uncle Tom, as an Illustration of Christianity."

The Christianity represented in the book was so far essential and unsectarian, that alike in the Protestant, Catholic, and Greek Church it has found sympathetic readers.

It has indeed been reported that "Uncle Tom's Cabin" has been placed in the Index of the Roman Catholic Church, but of this there may be a doubt, as when the author was in Rome she saw it in the hands of the common people, and no less in those of some of the highest officials in the Vatican, and heard from them in conversation expressions of warm sympathy with the purport of the work.

In France it was the testimony of colporteurs that the enthusiasm for the work awakened a demand for the Bible of Uncle Tom, and led to a sale of the Scriptures.

The accomplished translator of M. Charpentier's edition said to the author, that, by the researches necessary to translate correctly the numerous citations of Scripture in the work, she had been led to a most intimate knowledge of the sacred writings in French.

The witty scholar and *littérateur*, Heinrich Heine, speaking of his return to the Bible and its sources of consolation in the last years of his life, uses this language: —

"The reawakening of my religious feelings I owe to that holy book the Bible. Astonishing! that after I have whirled about all my life over all the dance-floors of philosophy, and yielded myself to all the orgies of the intellect, and paid my addresses to all possible systems, without satisfaction, like Messalina after a licentious night, I now find myself on the same stand-point where poor Uncle Tom stands, — on that of the Bible. I kneel down by my black brother in the same prayer! What a humiliation! With all my science I have come no farther than the poor ignorant negro who has scarce learned to spell. Poor Tom, indeed, seems to have seen deeper things in the holy book than I. . . . Tom, perhaps, understands them better than I, because more flogging occurs in them, — that is to say, those ceaseless blows of the whip which have æsthetically disgusted me in reading the Gospels and Acts. But a poor negro slave reads with his back, and understands better than we do. But I, who used to make citations from Homer, now begin to quote the Bible as Uncle Tom does." — *Vermischte Schriften*, p. 77.

The acute German in these words has touched the vital point in the catholic religious spirit of the book. "Uncle Tom's Cabin" shows that under circumstances of utter desolation and despair the religion of Christ can enable the poorest and most ignorant human being, not merely to submit, but to triumph, — that the soul of the lowest and weakest, by its aid, can become strong in superhuman virtue, and rise above every threat and terror and danger, in a sublime assurance of an ever-present love and an immortal life.

It is in this point of view that its wide circulation through all the languages of the earth may justly be a source of devout satisfaction.

Life has sorrows so hopeless, so dreadful, — so many drag through weary, joyless lives, — that a story which carries such a message as this can never cease to be a comforter.

The message is from Christ the Consoler, and too blessed is any one allowed by Him to carry it to the sorrowful children of men.

UNCLE TOM'S CABIN;

OR,

LIFE AMONG THE LOWLY.

CHAPTER I.

IN WHICH THE READER IS INTRODUCED TO A MAN OF HUMANITY.

LATE in the afternoon of a chilly day in February, two gentlemen were sitting alone over their wine, in a well-furnished dining parlor, in the town of P——, in Kentucky. There were no servants present, and the gentlemen, with chairs closely approaching, seemed to be discussing some subject with great earnestness.

For convenience' sake, we have said, hitherto, two *gentlemen*. One of the parties, however, when critically examined, did not seem, strictly speaking, to come under the species. He was a short thick-set man, with coarse commonplace features, and that swaggering air of pretension which marks a low man who is trying to elbow his way upward in the world. He was much overdressed, in a gaudy vest of many colors, a blue neckerchief, bedropped gayly with yellow spots, and arranged with a flaunting tie, quite in keeping with the general air of the man. His hands, large and coarse, were plentifully bedecked with rings; and he wore a heavy gold watch-chain, with a bundle of seals of portentous size, and a great variety of colors, attached to it, — which, in the ardor of conversation, he was in the habit of flourishing and jingling with evident satisfaction. His conversation was in free and easy defiance of Murray's Grammar, and was garnished at convenient intervals with various profane expressions, which not even the desire to be graphic in our account shall induce us to transcribe.

His companion, Mr. Shelby, had the appearance of a gentleman; and the arrangements of the house, and the general air of the housekeeping, indicated easy, and even opulent, circumstances. As we before stated, the two were in the midst of an earnest conversation.

"That is the way I should arrange the matter," said Mr. Shelby.

"I can't make trade that way, — I positively can't, Mr. Shelby," said the other, holding up a glass of wine between his eye and the light.

"Why, the fact is, Haley, Tom is an uncommon fellow; he is certainly worth that sum anywhere, — steady, honest, capable, manages my whole farm like a clock."

"You mean honest, as niggers go," said Haley, helping himself to a glass of brandy.

"No; I mean, really, Tom is a good, steady, sensible, pious fellow. He got religion at a camp-meeting, four years ago; and I believe he really *did* get it. I 've trusted him, since then, with everything I have, — money, house, horses, — and let him come and go round the country; and I always found him true and square in everything."

"Some folks don't believe there is pious niggers, Shelby," said Haley, with a candid flourish of his hand, "but *I do.* I had a fellow, now, in this yer last lot I took to Orleans, — 't was as good as a meetin', now, really, to hear that critter pray; and he was quite gentle and quiet like. He fetched me a good sum, too, for I bought him cheap of a man that was 'bliged to sell out; so I realized six hundred on him. Yes, I consider religion a valeyable thing in a nigger, when it 's the genuine article, and no mistake."

"Well, Tom 's got the real article, if ever a fellow had," rejoined the other. "Why, last fall, I let him go to Cincinnati alone, to do business for me, and bring home five hundred dollars. 'Tom,' says I to him, 'I trust you, because I think you 're a Christian, — I know you would n't cheat.' Tom comes back, sure enough; I knew he would. Some low fellows, they say, said to him, 'Tom, why don't you make tracks for Canada?'

'Ah, master trusted me, and I could n't,'—they told me about it. I am sorry to part with Tom, I must say. You ought to let him cover the whole balance of the debt; and you would, Haley, if you had any conscience."

"Well, I 've got just as much conscience as any man in business can afford to keep,—just a little, you know, to swear by, as 't were," said the trader, jocularly; "and, then, I 'm ready to do anything in reason to 'blige friends; but this yer, you see, is a leetle too hard on a fellow,—a leetle too hard." The trader sighed contemplatively, and poured out some more brandy.

"Well then, Haley, how will you trade?" said Mr. Shelby, after an uneasy interval of silence.

"Well, have n't you a boy or gal that you could throw in with Tom?"

"Hum!—none that I could well spare; to tell the truth, it 's only hard necessity makes me willing to sell at all. I don't like parting with any of my hands, that 's a fact."

Here the door opened, and a small quadroon boy, between four and five years of age, entered the room. There was something in his appearance remarkably beautiful and engaging. His black hair, fine as floss silk, hung in glossy curls about his round dimpled face, while a pair of large dark eyes, full of fire and softness, looked out from beneath the rich, long lashes, as he peered curiously into the apartment. A gay robe of scarlet and yellow plaid, carefully made and neatly fitted, set off to advantage the dark and rich style of his beauty; and a certain comic air of assurance, blended with bashfulness, showed that he had been not unused to being petted and noticed by his master.

"Hulloa, Jim Crow!" said Mr. Shelby, whistling, and snapping a bunch of raisins towards him, "pick that up, now!"

The child scampered, with all his little strength, after the prize, while his master laughed.

"Come here, Jim Crow," said he. The child came up, and the master patted the curly head, and chucked him under the chin.

"Now, Jim, show this gentleman how you can dance and sing." The boy commenced one of those wild, grotesque songs common among the negroes, in a rich, clear voice, accompanying his singing with many evolutions of the hands, feet, and whole body, all in perfect time to the music.

"Bravo!" said Haley, throwing him a quarter of an orange.

"Now, Jim, walk like old Uncle Cudjoe when he has the rheumatism," said his master.

Instantly the flexible limbs of the child assumed the appearance of deformity and distortion, as, with his back humped up, and his master's stick in his hand, he hobbled about the room, his childish face drawn into a doleful pucker, and spitting from right to left, in imitation of an old man.

Both gentlemen laughed uproariously.

"Now, Jim," said his master, "show us how old Elder Robbins leads the psalm." The boy drew his chubby face down to a formidable length, and commenced toning a psalm tune through his nose with imperturbable gravity.

"Hurrah! bravo! what a young un!" said Haley; "that chap 's a case, I 'll promise. Tell you what," said he, suddenly clapping his hand on Mr. Shelby's shoulder, "fling in that chap and I 'll settle the business, — I will. Come, now, if that an't doing the thing up about the rightest!"

At this moment, the door was pushed gently open, and a young quadroon woman, apparently about twenty-five, entered the room.

There needed only a glance from the child to her, to identify her as its mother. There was the same rich, full, dark eye, with its long lashes; the same ripples of silky black hair. The brown of her complexion gave way on the cheek to a perceptible flush, which deepened as she saw the gaze of the strange man fixed upon her in bold and undisguised admiration. Her dress was of the neatest possible fit, and set off to advantage her finely moulded shape; a delicately formed hand and a trim foot and ankle were items of appearance that did not escape the quick eye of the trader, well used to run up at a glance the points of a fine female article.

"Well, Eliza?" said her master, as she stopped and looked hesitatingly at him.

"I was looking for Harry, please, sir;" and the boy bounded toward her, showing his spoils, which he had gathered in the skirt of his robe.

"Well, take him away, then," said Mr. Shelby; and hastily she withdrew, carrying the child on her arm.

"By Jupiter," said the trader, turning to him in admiration, "there 's an article, now! You might make your fortune on that ar gal in Orleans, any day. I 've seen over a thousand, in my day, paid down for gals not a bit handsomer."

"I don't want to make my fortune on her," said Mr. Shelby dryly; and, seeking to turn the conversation, he uncorked a bottle of fresh wine, and asked his companion's opinion of it.

"Capital, sir, — first chop!" said the trader; then turning, and slapping his hand familiarly on Shelby's shoulder, he added, —

"Come, how will you trade about the gal? — what shall I say for her, — what 'll you take?"

"Mr. Haley, she is not to be sold," said Shelby. "My wife would not part with her for her weight in gold."

"Ay, ay! women always say such things, cause they han't no sort of calculation. Just show 'em how many watches, feathers, and trinkets one's weight in gold would buy, and that alters the case, *I* reckon."

"I tell you, Haley, this must not be spoken of; I say no, and I mean no," said Shelby, decidedly.

"Well, you 'll let me have the boy, though," said the trader; "you must own I 've come down pretty handsomely for him."

"What on earth can you want with the child?" said Shelby.

"Why, I 've got a friend that 's going into this yer branch of the business, — wants to buy up handsome boys to raise for the market. Fancy articles entirely, — sell for waiters, and so on, to rich 'uns, that can pay for handsome 'uns. It sets off one of yer great places, — a real handsome boy to open door, wait, and tend. They fetch a good sum; and this little devil is such a comical, musical concern, he 's just the article."

"I would rather not sell him," said Mr. Shelby, thoughtfully; "the fact is, sir, I 'm a humane man, and I hate to take the boy from his mother, sir."

"Oh, you do? — La! yes, — something of that ar natur. I understand, perfectly. It is mighty onpleasant getting on with women, sometimes. I al'ays hates these yer screechin', screamin' times. They are *mighty* onpleasant; but, as I manages business, I generally avoids 'em, sir. Now, what if you get the girl off for a day, or a week, or so; then the thing's done quietly, — all over before she comes home. Your wife might get her some ear-rings, or a new gown, or some such truck, to make up with her."

"I 'm afraid not."

"Lor bless ye, yes! These critters an't like white folks, you know; they gets over things, only manage right. Now, they say," said Haley, assuming a candid and confidential air, "that this kind o' trade is hardening to the feelings; but I never found it so. Fact is, I never could do things up the way some fellers manage the business. I 've seen 'em as would pull a woman's child out of her arms, and set him up to sell, and she screechin' like mad all the time; — very bad policy, — damages the article, — makes 'em quite unfit for service sometimes. I knew a real handsome gal once, in Orleans, as was entirely ruined by this sort o' handling. The fellow that was trading for her did n't want her baby; and she was one of your real high sort, when her blood was up. I tell you, she squeezed up her child in her arms, and talked, and went on real awful. It kinder makes my blood run cold to think on 't; and when they carried off the child, and locked her up, she jest went ravin' mad, and died in a week. Clear waste, sir, of a thousand dollars, jest for want of management, — there 's where 't is. It 's always best to do the humane thing, sir; that 's been *my* experience." And the trader leaned back in his chair, and folded his arms, with an air of virtuous decision, apparently considering himself a second Wilberforce.

The subject appeared to interest the gentleman deeply; for while Mr. Shelby was thoughtfully peeling an orange, Haley broke out afresh, with becoming diffidence, but as if actually driven by the force of truth to say a few words more.

"It don't look well, now, for a feller to be praisin' himself; but I say it jest because it 's the truth. I believe I 'm reckoned to bring in about the finest droves of niggers that is brought in, — at least, I 've been told so; if I have once, I reckon I have a hundred times, all in good case, — fat and likely, and I lose as few as any man in the business. And I lays it all to my management, sir; and humanity, sir, I may say, is the great pillar of *my* management."

Mr. Shelby did not know what to say, and so he said, "Indeed!"

"Now, I 've been laughed at for my notions, sir, and I 've been talked to. They an't pop'lar, and they an't common; but I stuck to 'em, sir; I 've stuck to 'em, and realized well on 'em; yes, sir, they have paid their passage, I may say," and the trader laughed at his joke.

There was something so piquant and original in these elucidations of humanity, that Mr. Shelby could not help laughing in company. Perhaps you laugh too, dear reader; but you know humanity comes out in a variety of strange forms nowadays, and there is no end to the odd things that humane people will say and do.

Mr. Shelby's laugh encouraged the trader to proceed.

"It 's strange now, but I never could beat this into people's heads. Now, there was Tom Loker, my old partner, down in Natchez; he was a clever fellow, Tom was, only the very devil with niggers, — on principle 't was, you see, for a better-hearted feller never broke bread; 't was his *system*, sir. I used to talk to Tom. 'Why, Tom,' I used to say, 'when your gals takes on and cry, what 's the use o' crackin' on 'em over the head, and knockin' on 'em round? It 's ridiculous,' says I, 'and don't do no sort o' good. Why, I don't see no harm in their cryin',' says I; 'it 's natur,' says I, 'and if natur can't blow off one way, it will another. Besides Tom,' says I, 'it jest spiles your gals; they get sickly and down in the mouth; and sometimes they gets ugly, — particular yallow gals do, — and it 's the devil and all gettin' on 'em broke in. Now,' says I, 'why can't you kinder coax 'em up, and speak 'em fair? Depend on it, Tom, a little humanity, thrown in along, goes a heap further than all your jawin' and crackin'; and it pays better,' says I, 'depend on 't.' But Tom could n't get the hang on 't; and he spiled so many for me, that I had to break off with him, though he was a good-hearted fellow, and as fair a business hand as is goin'."

"And do you find your ways of managing do the business better than Tom's?" said Mr. Shelby.

"Why, yes, sir, I may say so. You see, when I any ways can, I takes a leetle care about the onpleasant parts, like selling young uns and that, — get the gals out of the way, — out of sight, out of mind, you know, — and when it 's clean done, and can't be helped, they naturally gets used to it. 'Tan't, you know, as if it was white folks, that 's brought up in the way of 'spectin' to keep their children and wives, and all that. Niggers, you know, that 's fetched up properly han't no kind of 'spectations of no kind; so all these things comes easier."

"I 'm afraid mine are not properly brought up, then," said Mr. Shelby.

"S'pose not; you Kentucky folks spile your niggers. You mean well by 'em, but 'tan't no real kindness, arter all. Now, a nigger, you see, what 's got to be hacked and tumbled round the world, and sold to Tom, and Dick, and the Lord knows who, 'tan't no kindness to be givin' on him notions and expectations, and bringin' on him up too well, for the rough and tumble comes all the harder on him arter. Now, I venture to say, your niggers would be quite chop-fallen in a place where some of your plantation niggers would be singing and whooping like all possessed. Every man, you know, Mr. Shelby, naturally thinks well of his own ways; and I think I treat niggers just about as well as it 's ever worth while to treat 'em."

"It 's a happy thing to be satisfied," said Mr. Shelby, with a slight shrug, and some perceptible feelings of a disagreeable nature.

"Well," said Haley, after they had both silently picked their nuts for a season, "what do you say?"

"I 'll think the matter over, and talk with my wife," said Mr. Shelby. "Meantime, Haley, if you want the matter carried on in the quiet way you speak of, you 'd best not let your business in this neighborhood be known. It will get out among my boys, and it will not be a particularly quiet business getting away any of my fellows, if they know it, I 'll promise you."

"Oh, certainly, by all means, mum! of course. But I 'll tell you, I 'm in a devil of a hurry, and shall want to know, as soon as possible, what I may depend on," said he, rising and putting on his overcoat.

"Well, call up this evening, between six and seven, and you shall have my answer," said Mr. Shelby, and the trader bowed himself out of the apartment.

"I 'd like to have been able to kick the fellow down the steps," said he to himself, as he saw the door fairly closed, "with his impudent assurance; but he knows how much he has me at advantage. If anybody had ever said to me that I should sell Tom down south to one of those rascally traders, I should have said, 'Is thy servant a dog, that he should do this thing?' And now it must come, for aught I see. And Eliza's child, too! I know that I shall have some fuss with wife about that; and, for that matter, about Tom, too. So much for being in debt, — heigh-ho! The fellow sees his advantage, and means to push it."

Perhaps the mildest form of the system of slavery is to be seen in the State of Kentucky. The general prevalence of agricultural pursuits of a quiet and gradual nature, not requiring those periodic seasons of hurry and pressure that are called for in the business of more southern districts, makes the task of the negro a more healthful and reasonable one; while the master, content with a more gradual style of acquisition, has not those temptations to hard-heartedness which always overcome frail human nature when the prospect of sudden and rapid gain is weighed in the balance, with no heavier counterpoise than the interests of the helpless and unprotected.

Whoever visits some estates there, and witnesses the good-humored indulgence of some masters and mistresses, and the affectionate loyalty of some slaves, might be tempted to dream the oft-fabled poetic legend of a patriarchal institution, and all that; but over and above the scene there broods a portentous shadow, — the shadow of *law*. So long as the law considers all these human beings, with beating hearts and living affections, only as so many *things* belonging to a master, — so long as the failure, or misfortune, or imprudence, or death of the kindest owner may cause them any day to exchange a life of kind protection and indulgence for one of hopeless misery and toil, — so long it is impossible to make anything beautiful or desirable in the best-regulated administration of slavery.

Mr. Shelby was a fair average kind of man, good natured and

kindly, and disposed to easy indulgence of those around him, and there had never been a lack of anything which might contribute to the physical comfort of the negroes on his estate. He had, however, speculated largely and quite loosely; had involved himself deeply, and his notes to a large amount had come into the hands of Haley; and this small piece of information is the key to the preceding conversation.

Now, it had so happened that, in approaching the door, Eliza had caught enough of the conversation to know that a trader was making offers to her master for somebody.

She would gladly have stopped at the door to listen, as she came out; but her mistress just then calling, she was obliged to hasten away.

Still she thought she heard the trader make an offer for her boy; — could she be mistaken? Her heart swelled and throbbed, and she involuntarily strained him so tight that the little fellow looked up into her face in astonishment.

"Eliza, girl, what ails you to-day?" said her mistress, when Eliza had upset the wash-pitcher, knocked down the work-stand, and finally was abstractedly offering her mistress a long night-gown in place of the silk dress she had ordered her to bring from the wardrobe.

Eliza started. "Oh, missis!" she said, raising her eyes; then, bursting into tears, she sat down in a chair, and began sobbing.

"Why, Eliza, child! what ails you?" said her mistress.

"Oh, missis," said Eliza, "there 's been a trader talking with master in the parlor! I heard him."

"Well, silly child, suppose there has."

"Oh, missis, *do* you suppose mas'r would sell my Harry?" And the poor creature threw herself into a chair, and sobbed convulsively.

"Sell him! No, you foolish girl! You know your master never deals with those southern traders, and never means to sell any of his servants, as long as they behave well. Why, you silly child, who do you think would want to buy your Harry? Do you think all the world are set on him as you are, you goosie? Come, cheer up, and hook my dress. There now, put my back hair up in that pretty braid you learnt the other day, and don't go listening at doors any more."

"Well, but, missis, *you* never would give your consent — to — to" —

"Nonsense, child! to be sure I should n't. What do you talk sc for? I would as soon have one of my own children sold. But really, Eliza, you are getting altogether too proud of that little fellow. A man can't put his nose into the door, but you think he must be coming to buy him."

Reassured by her mistress's confident tone, Eliza proceeded nimbly and adroitly with her toilet, laughing at her own fears, as she proceeded.

Mrs. Shelby was a woman of a high class, both intellectually and morally. To that natural magnanimity and generosity of mind which one often marks as characteristic of the women of Kentucky, she added high moral and religious sensibility and principle, carried out with great energy and ability into practical results. Her husband, who made no professions to any particular religious character, nevertheless reverenced and respected the consistency of hers, and stood, perhaps, a little in awe of her opinion. Certain it was that he gave her unlimited scope in all her benevolent efforts for the comfort, instruction, and improvement of her servants, though he never took any decided part in them himself. In fact, if not exactly a believer in the doctrine of the efficiency of the extra good works of saints, he really seemed somehow or other to fancy that his wife had piety and benevolence enough for two, — to indulge a shadowy expectation of getting into heaven through her superabundance of qualities to which he made no particular pretension.

The heaviest load on his mind, after his conversation with the trader, lay in the foreseen necessity of breaking to his wife the arrangement contemplated, — meeting the importunities and opposition which he knew he should have reason to encounter.

Mrs. Shelby, being entirely ignorant of her husband's embarrassments, and knowing only the general kindliness of his temper, had been quite sincere in the entire incredulity with which she had met Eliza's suspicions. In fact, she dismissed the matter from her mind, without a second thought; and being occupied in preparations for an evening visit, it passed out of her thoughts entirely.

CHAPTER II.

THE MOTHER.

ELIZA had been brought up by her mistress, from girlhood, as a petted and indulged favorite.

The traveller in the south must often have remarked that peculiar air of refinement, that softness of voice and manner, which seems in many cases to be a particular gift to the quadroon and mulatto women. These natural graces in the quadroon are often united with beauty of the most dazzling kind, and in almost every case with a personal appearance prepossessing and agreeable. Eliza, such as we have described her, is not a fancy sketch, but taken from remembrance, as we saw her, years ago, in Kentucky. Safe under the protecting care of her mistress, Eliza had reached maturity without those temptations which make beauty so fatal an inheritance to a slave. She had been married to a bright and talented young mulatto man, who was a slave on a neighboring estate, and bore the name of George Harris.

This young man had been hired out by his master to work in a bagging factory, where his adroitness and ingenuity caused him to be considered the first hand in the place. He had invented a machine for the cleaning of the hemp, which, considering the education and circumstances of the inventor, displayed quite as much mechanical genius as Whitney's cotton-gin.[1]

He was possessed of a handsome person and pleasing manners, and was a general favorite in the factory. Nevertheless, as this young man was in the eye of the law not a man, but a thing, all these superior qualifications were subject to the control of a vulgar, narrow-minded, tyrannical master. This same gentleman, having heard of the fame of George's invention, took a ride over

[1] A machine of this description was really the invention of a young colored man in Kentucky.

to the factory, to see what this intelligent chattel had been about. He was received with great enthusiasm by the employer, who congratulated him on possessing so valuable a slave.

He was waited upon over the factory, shown the machinery by George, who, in high spirits, talked so fluently, held himself so erect, looked so handsome and manly, that his master began to feel an uneasy consciousness of inferiority. What business had his slave to be marching round the country, inventing machines, and holding up his head among gentlemen? He 'd soon put a stop to it. He 'd take him back, and put him to hoeing and digging, and "see if he 'd step about so smart." Accordingly, the manufacturer and all hands concerned were astounded when he suddenly demanded George's wages, and announced his intention of taking him home.

"But, Mr. Harris," remonstrated the manufacturer, "is n't this rather sudden?"

"What if it is? — is n't the man *mine?*"

"We would be willing, sir, to increase the rate of compensation."

"No object at all, sir. I don't need to hire any of my hands out, unless I 've a mind to."

"But, sir, he seems peculiarly adapted to this business."

"Dare say he may be; never was much adapted to anything that I set him about, I 'll be bound."

"But only think of his inventing this machine," interposed one of the workmen, rather unluckily.

"Oh, yes! — a machine for saving work, is it? He 'd invent that, I 'll be bound; let a nigger alone for that, any time. They are all labor-saving machines themselves, every one of 'em. No, he shall tramp!"

George had stood like one transfixed, at hearing his doom thus suddenly pronounced by a power that he knew was irresistible. He folded his arms, tightly pressed in his lips, but a whole volcano of bitter feelings burned in his bosom, and sent streams of fire through his veins. He breathed short, and his large dark eyes flashed like live coals; and he might have broken out into some dangerous ebullition, had not the kindly manufacturer touched him on the arm, and said, in a low tone, —

"Give way, George; go with him for the present. We 'll try to help you, yet."

The tyrant observed the whisper, and conjectured its import, though he could not hear what was said; and he inwardly strengthened himself in his determination to keep the power he possessed over his victim.

George was taken home, and put to the meanest drudgery of the farm. He had been able to repress every disrespectful word; but the flashing eye, the gloomy and troubled brow, were part of a natural language that could not be repressed, — indubitable signs, which showed too plainly that the man could not become a thing.

It was during the happy period of his employment in the factory that George had seen and married his wife. During that period, — being much trusted and favored by his employer, — he had free liberty to come and go at discretion. The marriage was highly approved of by Mrs. Shelby, who, with a little womanly complacency in match-making, felt pleased to unite her handsome favorite with one of her own class who seemed in every way suited to her; and so they were married in her mistress's great parlor, and her mistress herself adorned the bride's beautiful hair with orange-blossoms, and threw over it the bridal veil, which certainly could scarce have rested on a fairer head; and there was no lack of white gloves, and cake and wine, — of admiring guests to praise the bride's beauty, and her mistress's indulgence and liberality. For a year or two Eliza saw her husband frequently, and there was nothing to interrupt their happiness, except the loss of two infant children, to whom she was passionately attached, and whom she mourned with a grief so intense as to call for gentle remonstrance from her mistress, who sought with maternal anxiety, to direct her naturally passionate feelings within the bounds of reason and religion.

After the birth of little Harry, however, she had gradually become tranquillized and settled; and every bleeding tie and throbbing nerve, once more entwined with that little life, seemed to become sound and healthful, and Eliza was a happy woman up to the time that her husband was rudely torn from his kind employer, and brought under the iron sway of his legal owner.

The manufacturer, true to his word, visited Mr. Harris a week or two after George had been taken away. when, as he hoped, the heat of the occasion had passed away, and tried every possible inducement to lead him to restore him to his former employment.

"You need n't trouble yourself to talk any longer," said he, doggedly; "I know my own business, sir."

"I did not presume to interfere with it, sir. I only thought that you might think it for your interest to let your man to us on the terms proposed."

"Oh, I understand the matter well enough. I saw your winking and whispering, the day I took him out of the factory; but you don't come it over me that way. It 's a free country, sir; the man 's *mine*, and I do what I please with him, — that 's it!"

And so fell George's last hope; — nothing before him but a life of toil and drudgery, rendered more bitter by every little smarting vexation and indignity which tyrannical ingenuity could devise.

A very humane jurist once said, The worst use you can put a man to is to hang him. No: there is another use that a man can be put to that is WORSE!

CHAPTER III.

THE HUSBAND AND FATHER.

MRS. SHELBY had gone on her visit, and Eliza stood in the veranda, rather dejectedly looking after the retreating carriage, when a hand was laid on her shoulder. She turned, and a bright smile lighted up her fine eyes.

"George, is it you? How you frightened me! Well! I am so glad you 's come! Missis is gone to spend the afternoon; so come into my little room, and we 'll have the time all to ourselves."

Saying this, she drew him into a neat little apartment opening on the veranda. where she generally sat at her sewing, within call of her mistress.

"How glad I am! — why don't you smile? — and look at Harry, — how he grows." The boy stood shyly regarding his father through his curls, holding close to the skirts of his mother's dress. "Is n't he beautiful?" said Eliza, lifting his long curls and kissing him.

"I wish he 'd never been born!" said George, bitterly. "I wish I 'd never been born myself!"

Surprised and frightened, Eliza sat down, leaned her head on her husband's shoulder, and burst into tears.

"There now, Eliza, it 's too bad for me to make you feel so, poor girl!" said he, fondly; "it 's too bad. Oh, how I wish you never had seen me, — you might have been happy!"

"George! George! how can you talk so? What dreadful thing has happened, or is going to happen? I 'm sure we 've been very happy, till lately."

"So we have, dear," said George. Then drawing his child on his knee, he gazed intently on his glorious dark eyes, and passed his hands through his long curls.

"Just like you, Eliza; and you are the handsomest woman I

ever saw, and the best one I ever wish to see; but, oh, I wish I 'd never seen you, nor you me!"

"Oh, George, how can you!"

"Yes, Eliza, it 's all misery, misery, misery! My life is bitter as wormwood; the very life is burning out of me. I 'm a poor, miserable, forlorn drudge; I shall only drag you down with me, that 's all. What 's the use of our trying to do anything, trying to know anything, trying to be anything? What 's the use of living? I wish I was dead!"

"Oh, now, dear George, that is really wicked! I know how you feel about losing your place in the factory, and you have a hard master; but pray be patient, and perhaps something" —

"Patient!" said he, interrupting her; "have n't I been patient? Did I say a word when he came and took me away, for no earthly reason, from the place where everybody was kind to me? I 'd paid him truly every cent of my earnings, — and they all say I worked well."

"Well, it *is* dreadful," said Eliza; "but, after all, he is your master, you know."

"My master! and who made him my master? That 's what I think of, — what right has he to me? I 'm a man as much as he is. I 'm a better man than he is. I know more about business than he does; I am a better manager than he is; I can read better than he can; I can write a better hand, — and I 've learned it all myself, and no thanks to him, — I 've learned it in spite of him; and now what right has he to make a dray-horse of me? — to take me from things I can do, and do better than he can, and put me to work that any horse can do? He tries to do it; he says he 'll bring me down and humble me, and he puts me to just the hardest, meanest, and dirtiest work, on purpose!"

"Oh, George! George! you frighten me! Why, I never heard you talk so; I 'm afraid you 'll do something dreadful. I don't wonder at your feelings at all; but oh, do be careful — do, do — for my sake, — for Harry's!"

"I have been careful, and I have been patient, but it 's growing worse and worse; flesh and blood can't bear it any longer; — every chance he can get to insult and torment me, he takes. I thought I could do my work well, and keep on

2

quiet, and have some time to read and learn out of work hours; but the more he sees I can do, the more he loads on. He says that though I don't say anything, he sees I 've got the devil in me, and he means to bring it out; and one of these days it will come out in a way that he won't like, or I 'm mistaken!"

"Oh, dear! what shall we do?" said Eliza, mournfully.

"It was only yesterday," said George, "as I was busy loading stones into a cart, that young Mas'r Tom stood there, slashing his whip so near the horse that the creature was frightened. I asked him to stop, as pleasant as I could, — he just kept right on. I begged him again, and then he turned on me, and began striking me. I held his hand, and then he screamed and kicked and ran to his father, and told him that I was fighting him. He came in a rage, and said he 'd teach me who was my master; and he tied me to a tree, and cut switches for young master, and told him that he might whip me till he was tired; — and he did do it! If I don't make him remember it, some time!" and the brow of the young man grew dark, and his eyes burned with an expression that made his young wife tremble. "Who made this man my master? That 's what I want to know!" he said.

"Well," said Eliza mournfully, "I always thought that I must obey my master and mistress, or I could n't be a Christian."

"There is some sense in it, in your case; they have brought you up like a child, fed you, clothed you, indulged you, and taught you, so that you have a good education; that is some reason why they should claim you. But I have been kicked and cuffed and sworn at, and at the best only let alone; and what do I owe? I 've paid for all my keeping a hundred times over. I *won't* bear it. No, I *won't!*" he said, clenching his hand with a fierce frown.

Eliza trembled, and was silent. She had never seen her husband in this mood before; and her gentle system of ethics seemed to bend like a reed in the surges of such passions.

"You know poor little Carlo, that you gave me," added George; "the creature has been about all the comfort that I 've had. He has slept with me nights, and followed me around days, and kind o' looked at me as if he understood how